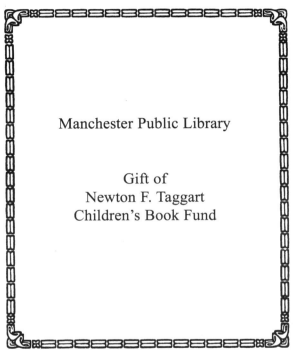

BLUE BANNER
BIOGRAPHY

# Russell
# WESTBROOK

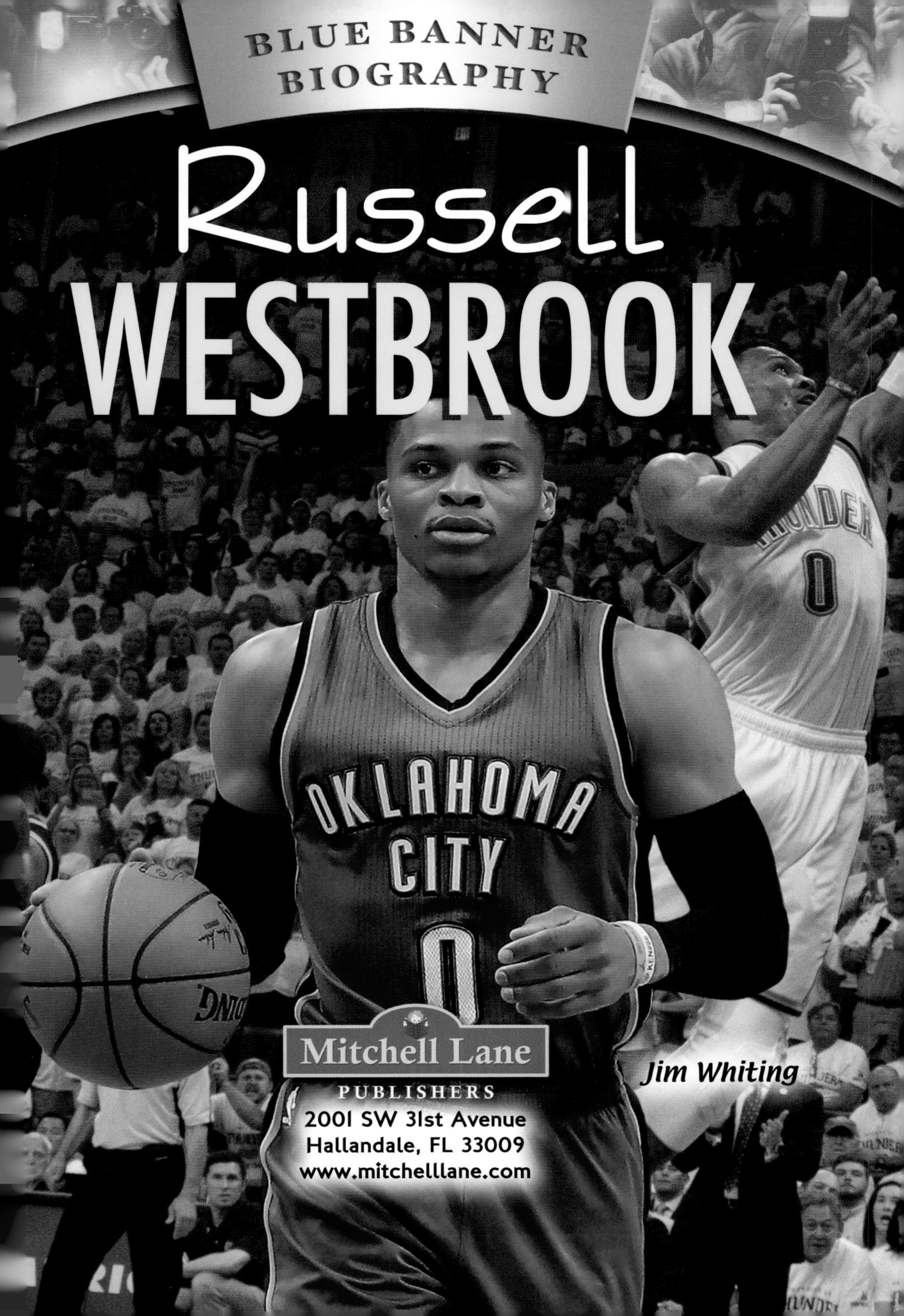

Mitchell Lane
PUBLISHERS
2001 SW 31st Avenue
Hallandale, FL 33009
www.mitchelllane.com

*Jim Whiting*

**Mitchell Lane**
PUBLISHERS

Printing     1        2        3        4        5        6        7        8        9

## Blue Banner Biographies

| | | |
|---|---|---|
| 5 Seconds of Summer | Hope Solo | Miguel Tejada |
| Abby Wambach | Ice Cube | Mike Trout |
| Adele | Jamie Foxx | Nancy Pelosi |
| Alicia Keys | James Harden | Natasha Bedingfield |
| Allen Iverson | Ja Rule | Nicki Minaj |
| Ashanti | Jason Derulo | One Direction |
| Ashlee Simpson | Jay-Z | Orianthi |
| Ashton Kutcher | Jennifer Hudson | Orlando Bloom |
| Avril Lavigne | Jennifer Lopez | P. Diddy |
| Blake Lively | Jessica Simpson | Peyton Manning |
| Blake Shelton | JJ Watt | Pharrell Williams |
| Bow Wow | J. K. Rowling | Pit Bull |
| Brett Favre | John Legend | Prince William |
| Britney Spears | Justin Berfield | Queen Latifah |
| CC Sabathia | Justin Timberlake | Robert Downey Jr. |
| Carrie Underwood | Kanye West | Ron Howard |
| Chris Brown | Kate Hudson | Russell Westbrook |
| Chris Daughtry | Keith Urban | Russell Wilson |
| Christina Aguilera | Kelly Clarkson | Sean Kingston |
| Clay Aiken | Kenny Chesney | Selena |
| Cole Hamels | Ke$ha | Shia LaBeouf |
| Condoleezza Rice | Kevin Durant | Shontelle Layne |
| Corbin Bleu | Kristen Stewart | Soulja Boy Tell 'Em |
| Daniel Radcliffe | Lady Gaga | Stephenie Meyer |
| David Ortiz | Lance Armstrong | Taylor Swift |
| David Wright | Leona Lewis | T.I. |
| Derek Hough | Lindsay Lohan | Timbaland |
| Derek Jeter | LL Cool J | Tim McGraw |
| Drew Brees | Ludacris | Toby Keith |
| Dwyane Wade | Luke Bryan | Usher |
| Eminem | Mariah Carey | Vanessa Anne Hudgens |
| Eve | Mario | The Weeknd |
| Fergie | Mary J. Blige | Will.i.am |
| Flo Rida | Mary-Kate and Ashley Olsen | Zac Efron |
| Gwen Stefani | Megan Fox | |

**Library of Congress Cataloging-in-Publication Data**
Names: Whiting, Jim, author.
Title: Russell Westbrook / by Jim Whiting.
Description: Hallandale, FL : Mitchell Lane Publishers, [2018] | Series: A Blue Banner Biography |
    Includes bibliographical references and index.
Identifiers: LCCN 2017024494 | ISBN 9781680201338 (library bound)
Subjects: LCSH: Westbrook, Russell, 1988– —Juvenile literature. | Basketball players—United
    States—Biography—Juvenile literature.
Classification: LCC GV884.W44 G34 2018 | DDC 796.323092 [B] —dc23
LC record available at https://lccn.loc.gov/2017024494

eBook ISBN: 978-1-68020-1-345

**ABOUT THE AUTHOR:** Jim Whiting is a lifelong sports participant and fan. He has written dozens of books and hundreds of magazine and newspaper articles about a wide variety of sports. Overall, he is the author of more than 200 books for young readers and has edited at least 500 more. He lives in Washington State.

Blue Banner Biography

Oklahoma City Thunder guard Russell Westbrook drives the lane before passing to a teammate in a game against the Denver Nuggets on April 9, 2017. Later that night he would break one of the oldest records in National Basketball Association (NBA) history.

# Triple-Double! (42 Times!)

**F**our minutes and 17 seconds remained in the Oklahoma City Thunder's game against the Denver Nuggets. Thunder guard Russell Westbrook drove down the right side of the lane, then passed the basketball to teammate Semaj Christon in the corner. Christon sank a three-point shot. The fans in Denver's Pepsi Center leaped to their feet. They cheered and applauded even though the other team had scored. The game had to be halted for a few moments.

They had good reason for their excitement. It was April 9, 2017. Russell had just broken one of the oldest records in the National Basketball Association (NBA). It was his 42nd triple-double of the season. A triple-double means that a player has achieved double figures in three of five categories: points, **rebounds**, **assists**, blocked shots, and steals. The most common triple-double includes points, rebounds, and assists. In this game, Russell already had double figures in points and rebounds by halftime. The pass to Christon was his 10th assist of the game and set the new mark. He put a huge exclamation mark on the

*Russell caps his historic evening by sinking a buzzer-beating three-point shot to give his team a two-point victory.*

evening when he sank a 30-foot shot in the final seconds to win the game.

Basketball legend Oscar Robertson set the previous record of 41 triple-doubles in the 1961–1962 season. That was 55 years ago! Russell also became the only player besides Robertson to average a triple-double for the entire season. He led the league in scoring with an average of 31.6 points per game, to go along with 10.7 rebounds and 10.4 assists.

Triple-doubles are difficult to achieve. It takes a special kind of player. They must be highly skilled in all aspects of the sport of basketball and are at the center of the action almost every time their team has the ball. There's another factor at work. A player is in control of his own scoring and rebounding. But when he passes the ball to a teammate, he only gets credit for an assist if the teammate makes the shot. One sign of the difficulty is that NBA

*Russell's teammates rush to congratulate him after his shot wins the game for the Thunder.*

teams played a total of 1,230 games in the 2016–17 season. Only 22 other players besides Russell had one or more games with a triple-double.

Russell's pursuit of the record had the full support of his teammates. "He's making big plays," said forward Enes Kanter. "That's what a big player does. He's taking a lot of responsibility and doing amazing things. And he's making everybody better around him."

Many people had regarded Robertson's record as difficult to break as other legendary sports records such as Joe DiMaggio's 56-game hitting streak, Wilt Chamberlain's 100 points in a single basketball game, or Ron Hunt of the Montreal Expos being hit by a pitch 50 times during one season (ouch!). En route to the record, Russell had several especially significant performances.

- On March 23, he scored "only" 18 points against the Philadelphia 76ers, along with 14 assists and 11 rebounds. But he was a perfect 6-for-6 in shooting field goals and 6-for-6 from the free throw line. That made him the first-ever NBA player to achieve a triple-double without missing any shots.
- On March 29, Russell had 57 points against the Orlando Magic as part of his 38th triple-double. It was the highest point total in a triple-double in NBA history. It was also significant from a team point of view. Russell helped his team overcome a 21-point **deficit** in the third quarter as they went on to win 114–106. It was the biggest comeback in Thunder history.
- In separate games on April 2, Russell and LeBron James of the Cleveland Cavaliers each scored 40 points in racking up triple-doubles. The last time two players scored 40 points as part of triple-doubles on the same day was in 1975.

*Before the Thunder's home game on April 12, 2017, Oscar Robertson presents Russell Westbrook with an award for breaking his single-season triple-double record.*

- Both Russell and James Harden of the Houston Rockets had two triple-double games in which they scored at least 50 points. It is the only time in NBA history that two players have done that.

Russell's amazing accomplishment made him one of the frontrunners for the league's Most Valuable Player (MVP) Award. The winner was announced in late June. It was Russell!

# *Little Guy Grows Up and Makes Good*

**R**ussell Westbrook III was born on November 12, 1988 in Long Beach, California to Russell Westbrook Jr. and Shannon Horton. The youngster discovered basketball at age seven while watching his father play. His father's games were about as far from the NBA as one could get. The court was at a rundown recreational center in Los Angeles. That didn't matter to young Russell. He instantly fell in love with the game.

His parents thought that basketball was a positive **pastime**. They didn't want Russell or his younger brother Raynard wandering aimlessly around the city. As Russell told *NewsOK* in 2011, "I was never that type. My family put that in me at a young age. Nothing good happens in the streets."

Russell and his father spent many hours playing the game together. Russell practiced shooting from every spot on the court. He normally shot 500 times or even more in a single day. Often he would shoot several times from the exact same spot, then move a couple of inches and do the same thing. Russell never got bored or felt pressured. From the beginning he always wanted to be as good as he could.

*Russell Westbrook poses with his family when he is inducted into the Oklahoma Hall of Fame on November 17, 2016. From left, his brother Ray, his wife Nina, Russell, his mother Shannon, and his father Russell.*

It soon became apparent that Russell had inherited his father's athletic abilities. Both of them could leap into the air like few other players.

But Russell didn't get his eventual height of 6 feet, 3 inches from his father, who stands just 5 feet, 8 inches tall. As a freshman at Leuzinger High School in Lawndale, Russell was the same height as his father and weighed just 140 pounds. Luckily for Russell, his grandfather and several other family members were over 6 feet.

Russell's dad told *NewsOK* he realized just how serious his son was about his athletic goals during that freshman year when the family sat down for Thanksgiving dinner. "He said 'Dad, I know it's Thanksgiving. But I want to shoot. Let's go shoot.' I looked at my wife. I looked at Ray. I said, 'Let's go shoot.' And we put it in like it was a normal day."

Despite his lack of height, Russell impressed his Leuzinger teammates. Future NBA player Dorell Wright shared his memories of Russell as a freshman with *NewsOK*. "I still got video from my senior year when you see Russ at the end of the bench, big ol' clothes on, little as I don't know what, with some 15s [size shoes] on," Wright said. "He was always the smallest one but he was always the toughest one." Despite his toughness, Russell didn't become a starter until his junior year.

By then he had undergone what some people regard as the most formative experience of his life. His teammate and closest friend, Khelcey Barrs III, died during a pickup game. He had an enlarged heart no one knew about. The two of them lived across the street from each other. They had dreamed of winning a state championship and going on to play college ball together. Writing in 2017 about Khelcey's death, Mike Piellucci of Vice Sports noted that

> Former teammates say that Westbrook became even more determined, playing as though he could glue the pieces back together if he just tried hard enough. . . . Now, as Westbrook seemingly bends the league to his every whim, [former Leuzinger assistant coach Chris] Young says he knows exactly where the inexhaustible supply of **resolve** comes from. 'Russell is living his dream for his friend. I believe Khelcey's energy is in Russell.'

Even today, Russell wears a "KB3" wrist bracelet during every game in honor of Khelcey. "When he passed, it just made me think about life and how every time I step on the floor I have to give it my all because every time he played he gave 100 percent," Russell explained to ESPN's Arash Markazi. "You can't take life for granted."

He had another **motivation** for playing hard. "I wasn't that good," Westbrook said bluntly to Lee Jenkins of *Sports Illustrated* in 2016. "I really wasn't. All I cared about was that my parents didn't have to pay for college." To achieve that goal, Russell had to stand out to recruiters. His size made that difficult at first. But just before his senior season, he experienced a growth spurt. This new height added to his self-confidence and helped him lead Leuzinger to a 25–4 record. Russell averaged 25 points and nearly 9 rebounds per game. He was named third-team All-State. But even those numbers didn't attract much attention from colleges. Russell felt disrespected.

Soon afterward, UCLA point guard Jordan Farmar entered the NBA draft. His backup, Darren Collison, would replace him in the starting lineup. So UCLA needed someone to back up Collison. The school was only about 15 miles from Leuzinger. Its basketball staff had been quietly watching Russell. They liked what they saw.

Head coach Ben Howland wanted to see for himself. He arrived at the Leuzinger gym at 6:30 one morning. The only other person in the building was a thin youngster pushing a broom. Moments later Leuzinger coach Reggie Morris joined Howland. Howland asked when he could see Russell. Morris pointed to the kid behind the broom. When Russell was done, he gathered his teammates and organized their warmup drills.

"My first introduction to Russell Westbrook was as a leader," Howland told Chris Palmer of *Bleacher Report*. "It was pretty impressive." Howland offered him a scholarship. Russell happily accepted.

In his first game as a UCLA Bruin, Russell pushes the ball upcourt against Cal Poly Pomona. "Freshman Russell Westbrook is the real deal," wrote Bruin Basketball Report after the game. "Westbrook excelled defensively. He is athletic, quick, and very physical."

# *From Bruin to the Big Time*

*C*ollege was a new challenge for Russell. He took his studies seriously. Dr. Mary Corey, a UCLA history professor, told *Bleacher Report*, "He was humble and friendly and unswaggery. He had a real **intellectual** curiosity."

It also helped Russell's adjustment to college life that he met a young woman named Nina Earl. Like him, she had been recruited to play basketball for the school. The pair instantly became friends and soon started dating.

Russell had hoped to continue wearing jersey #4, his high school number. But one of his new teammates already had it. After some thought, he decided on 0. "You go with the zero when you've been through something and you are looking to get a new beginning," he explained to Lee Jenkins in *The New York Times*. "It helps you get going again. It helps you get the swag[ger] back."

It took a while for Russell to get his swag back. He didn't play much during his freshman year. He averaged about nine minutes on the court, with an average of just over three points and less than a rebound per game. Hardly anyone outside of the UCLA community paid any attention to him. The eyes of the college basketball world were focused on the University of Texas, where another freshman was having one of the greatest seasons ever recorded by a first-year player. Kevin Durant averaged 36 minutes a game while scoring 26 points and pulling down 11 rebounds. No one could have foreseen that these two young players would soon become one of the NBA's most potent one-two scoring punches.

Russell didn't want to spend another season on the bench. He worked hard during the summer in the weight room. When he finished there, he played pickup games that included top pros such as Kobe Bryant and Kevin Garnett. He played so hard and moved so fast around the court that no one wanted to guard him. Howland couldn't attend those games, but he got plenty of feedback from participants. "They'd just come up to me and say, 'Wow," he told *Bleacher Report*. "He just blew up that summer."

Once again all of Russell's hard work paid off. He moved into the UCLA starting lineup as shooting guard the following year and logged more minutes than any other Bruin since at least 1979. Russell averaged 13 points, four rebounds, and four assists per game. He was named the Defensive Player of the Year in the Pac-10 (now Pac-12) and to the All-Pac-10 Third Team. UCLA went 35-4 and advanced to the NCAA Final Four for the third year in a row. But they lost to Memphis in the semi-finals.

After the season ended, Russell made a big decision. He told Howland that he wanted to enter the 2008 NBA draft. Howland was unsure. He knew Russell was a good player. But he thought he needed more time to develop his skills at the college level. Howland thought Russell's chances of becoming one of the top picks in the draft would be greater with that extra time. But Russell did not change his mind.

The work ethic his father had instilled in him still ran strong. As soon as Russell declared himself **eligible** for the draft, he began training every day with Rob McClanaghan, one of the country's best-known basketball skills trainers. McClanaghan's biggest challenge was getting his **client** to slow down when necessary. Pacing yourself is important, he told Russell.

One way in which Westbrook didn't pace himself was in striving for improvement. He knew that the best way to get better was dedicated practice. McClanaghan told *Bleacher Report*, "He wanted to go seven days a week."

On the night of the draft, Russell was especially nervous. He was one of the players the NBA had invited to sit backstage in what is called the "green room" while the draft went on. That way they could come out and be introduced right away. Russell was afraid that he would be the only player remaining in the green room when the draft was complete.

The Seattle SuperSonics had the fourth overall pick. Going into the draft, several people in the team's front office believed that drafting a big man was their top priority. When it was the SuperSonics' turn, 7-0 Stanford sophomore Brooke Lopez was available. With Durant, he would form a formidable frontcourt if the team chose him. But general manager Sam Presti announced Russell's name instead.

Presti had done his homework. Before the draft, he called many of the players who were likely to be chosen and asked a simple question: "Who's the toughest player you faced this season?" Nearly all of them replied, "Russell Westbrook."

Presti's decision surprised many people. Some were openly critical. "It doesn't make sense," said college basketball analyst Dick Vitale. "Seattle will look back on this and realize they made a big, big mistake." Perhaps no

NBA commissioner David Stern shakes hands with Russell after the Seattle SuperSonics made Russell the fourth overall pick in the 2008 NBA draft. Russell would soon trade his SuperSonics cap for an Oklahoma City one.

one was more surprised, though, than Russell. He may even have felt like pinching himself to make sure it was really happening. "I never thought I was going to play in the NBA," he told *Bleacher Report*. "A lot of people who are in the NBA now have been good since they were eight. I wasn't good until I was 17."

But it was really happening. After all his hard work, Russell had finally made it into the NBA.

# CHAPTER 4

# *All-Star*

**A** week after the draft, the SuperSonics moved to Oklahoma City and took on their new name of Thunder. Russell began playing alongside Durant. Durant had joined the team the previous year and been named Rookie of the Year. The pair quickly became one of the NBA's most powerful duos.

One reason they worked so well together may have been how different they are. While Durant is known for his calm demeanor, Russell quickly gained a **reputation** for intensity on the court. In a sign of things to come, he recorded his first triple-double on March 2, 2009. By then, he had become a fixture in the starting lineup. Durant told Mike Baldwin of *NewsOK*, "The games where he got nine, 10, or 11 assists, we won pretty big. That shows how much an impact he has on this team. He had a great year. I'm excited for him." So were the NBA's head coaches, who named him to the All-Rookie First Team. But despite Russell's stellar play, the Thunder won just 23 games.

Russell and Durant led the team to a 50–32 mark in 2009–10. It was one of the largest turnarounds in NBA

As a member of the Thunder, Russell teamed with Kevin Durant to form one of the NBA's most powerful one-two punches for eight seasons.

history. The Thunder made the playoffs for the first time in five years. Though they lost to the Los Angeles Lakers in the first round, Oklahoma City was a team on the rise.

The improvement continued in 2010–11. The Thunder won 55 games and advanced to the Western Conference semi-finals before losing to the Dallas Mavericks, four games to one. Russell averaged 22 points a game and played in the All-Star Game. He was named to the All-NBA Second Team for the first of three seasons in a row.

Russell and Durant powered the team to the NBA Finals in the 2011-12 season. But they lost to LeBron James and the powerful Miami Heat.

The Thunder won 60 games the following season. It was their highest victory total since 1997–98 when the team was still in Seattle. Russell averaged 23 points and more than 7 assists per game. Oklahoma City entered the playoffs as the Western Conference's top seed. Unfortunately, the injury bug bit Russell in the knee. Without him, the Thunder lost to the Memphis Grizzlies in the second round, four games to one.

> *Russell and Durant powered the team to the NBA Finals in the 2011-12 season. But they lost to LeBron James and the powerful Miami Heat.*

With the knee still bothering him, Russell missed nearly half of the following season. He also missed 15 games in 2014–15. Despite this, he led the league in scoring with an average of 28 points a game, was named MVP of the All-Star Game, and All-NBA Second Team. But the

Thunder didn't make the playoffs even though they won 45 games.

Oklahoma City bounced back the following season. They improved to 55 wins as Westbrook and Durant fired on all cylinders. Against the Orlando Magic, they became the first teammates in 20 seasons to both score 40 points in the same game. In the playoffs, they took a 3–1 lead over the Golden State Warriors in the Western Conference Finals. The Warriors had just set an NBA record by winning 73 games in the regular season. But the Thunder couldn't close out the series, losing each of the next three games by just a few points and being eliminated.

*Oklahoma City general manager Sam Presti and Russell hold a press conference in August, 2016 after Russell signed a contract extension with the Thunder.*

*Kevin Durant congratulates Russell for winning the Most Valuable Player Award at the 2016 All-Star Game. Russell scored 31 points as he became the first-ever player to win the award in back-to-back seasons.*

Much, much worse was in store for Thunder fans. A little more than a month later, Durant announced that he was leaving the team. He signed with the Warriors.

*Russell shoots over James Harden in a 2017 playoff game against the Houston Rockets. Harden, Russell's main competition for the MVP award that season, helped his team defeat the Thunder 113–109 in the game. The Rockets also won the series, four games to one.*

# *Staying Put, and Giving Back*

Oklahoma City fans were jolted when Durant left. They braced themselves for what they thought would be a double dose of disappointment. Without Durant, they thought, the Thunder would have no chance at winning an NBA title. So they thought Russell would follow him and play for a team that would give him a better chance for a championship ring. He would also get more media exposure if he joined a team in a larger city, such as Los Angeles or New York.

Instead, Russell signed a contract extension. That set the stage for his historic season. When it began, he had 37 career triple-doubles. That placed him ninth on the all-time list. When it was over, he had moved up to fourth with 79. He passed three of the league's greatest-ever players during the season: LeBron James, Larry Bird, and Wilt Chamberlain.

When Russell broke his record, Robertson graciously wrote, "I could not be happier for him. Congratulations to Russell Westbrook on a magnificent season! . . . If he stays healthy, there's no reason he couldn't eventually break my career record of 181 triple-double games."

With Russell's leadership, Oklahoma City did better than many people had predicted when Durant left. They won 47 games and earned the sixth seed in the playoffs. The Thunder faced the Houston Rockets and Harden. He and Russell were the favorites for the league's MVP award, and it was by far the most anticipated first-round matchup. Russell did his best. He averaged more than 37 points a game. But it wasn't enough. The Rockets had too much overall team depth. The Thunder only managed a single win.

With all his fame and fortune, Russell works at giving back. He laid the roots for his generosity when he was in high school. He did chores for Khelcey Barrs's grandmother after his friend's death.

In 2012, he started the Russell Westbrook Why Not? Foundation. According to the organization's website, its mission "is to inspire the lives of children, empower them to ask 'Why Not?' and teach them to never give up. The foundation works to help children that are facing hardships of any kind and when faced with that adversity fight to succeed and to never give up." Russell often appears at the foundation's events, such as the Why Not? Bowl at a local bowling alley and serving food at Thanksgiving dinners for needy families.

The foundation's name comes from Russell's self-confidence and drive to succeed when others doubted him. He would always respond, "Why not?" So in addition to his KB3 wristbands, he has one saying "Why not?"

Russell married his girlfriend Nina in 2015. Soon afterward, he made the largest donation to UCLA the university has ever received from a former player. The funds went toward the construction of a basketball center for future Bruins. "I loved my time at UCLA and jumped at the opportunity to give back to the University that

*Russell serves up food in 2015 during the annual Thanksgiving dinner that his Why Not? Foundation sponsors for families in the Oklahoma City area.*

provided me with amazing opportunities and great memories," Russell said in a statement.

Following Durant's decision to leave the Thunder, many people wondered if Russell would stay or go. He explained his decision to stay to Daniel Riley of *GQ* magazine. "It's a new situation [without Durant], but my mind-set stays the same," he said. "The best thing I can do is stay true to myself. . . . It was just very simple I wasn't trying to figure out if I was leaving or not. I was happy where—I am happy where—I'm at."

Thunder fans are happy too. They look forward to Russell leading the charge toward an NBA title.

| | |
|---|---|
| 1988 | Russell Westbrook is born in Long Beach, California on November 12. |
| 2006 | Russell leads his Leuzinger High School team to a 25–4 record; UCLA coach Ben Howland offers him a scholarship. |
| 2007 | As part of the Bruins, Russell makes it to the NCAA Final Four. |
| 2008 | Russell becomes a starter and helps UCLA to the NCAA Final Four; he declares for the NBA Draft; the Seattle SuperSonics make him the fourth overall pick just before moving to Oklahoma City and becoming the Thunder. |
| 2009 | Russell scores his first triple-double and is named to the All-Rookie First Team. |
| 2012 | Russell helps lead the Thunder to the NBA Finals; he establishes the Russell Westbrook Why Not? Foundation. |
| 2015 | Russell is named All-Star Game MVP; he marries longtime girlfriend Nina Earl; he makes the largest donation in history from any former Bruins player to UCLA. |
| 2016 | Russell is named All-Star Game MVP for the second time. |
| 2017 | Russell breaks Oscar Robertson's 55-year-old record for triple-doubles in a season; he is named NBA's Most Valuable Player. |

# CAREER STATS

| Season | Team | GP | GS | PPG | RPG | APG | SPG |
|--------|------|-----|-----|-----|------|------|-----|
| 2008-09 | OK City | 82 | 64 | 15.3 | 4.9 | 5.3 | 1.3 |
| 2009-10 | OK City | 82 | 82 | 16.1 | 4.9 | 8.0 | 1.3 |
| 2010-11 | OK City | 82 | 82 | 21.0 | 4.6 | 8.2 | 1.9 |
| 2011-12 | OK City | 66 | 66 | 23.6 | 4.6 | 5.5 | 1.7 |
| 2012-13 | OK City | 82 | 82 | 23.2 | 5.2 | 7.4 | 1.8 |
| 2013-14 | OK City | 46 | 46 | 21.8 | 5.7 | 6.9 | 1.9 |
| 2014-15 | OK City | 67 | 67 | 28.1 | 7.3 | 8.6 | 2.1 |
| 2015-16 | OK City | 80 | 80 | 23.5 | 7.8 | 10.4 | 2.0 |
| 2016-17 | OK City | 81 | 81 | 31.6 | 10.7 | 10.4 | 1.6 |
| Career | | 668 | 650 | 22.7 | 6.2 | 7.9 | 1.7 |

**Legend:** G = games played, GS = games started, PPG = points per game,
RPG = rebounds per game, APG = assists per game, SPG = steals per game
**Source:** http://www.espn.com/nba/player/stats/_/id/3468/russell-westbrook

# GLOSSARY

**assist** (uh-SIST) — passing the ball to a teammate who scores
**client** (CLY-uhnt) — a person who uses the professional services of
   an expert in a particular area
**deficit** (DEH-fuh-suht) — the amount that a team is losing by
**eligible** (EL-uh-juh-buhl) — able to be chosen
**intellectual** (in-tuh-LEK-choo-uhl) — relating to mental capacity
**motivation** (moe-tih-VAY-shun) — desire or willingness to do
   something
**pastime** (PASS-tyme) — activity
**rebound** (REE-bownd) — controlling the ball after a missed shot
**reputation** (rep-yoo-TAY-shuhn) — the overall opinion of a person
   by a group of people
**resolve** (ree-ZOHLV) — determination

# FURTHER READING

**Books**

Doeden, Matt. *Russell Westbrook*. Minneapolis, MN: Lerner Publications, 2017.

Geoffreys, Clayton. *Russell Westbrook: The Inspiring Story of One of Basketball's Premier Point Guards*. Seattle, WA: CreateSpace Independent Publishing Platform, 2014.

Hall, Brian. *Russell Westbrook*. Fort Wayne, IN: SportsZone, 2016.

Lowe, Jordan. *Russell Westbrook: The Incredible Story of Russell Westbrook – One of Basketball's Greatest Players*. Seattle, WA: CreateSpace Independent Publishing Platform, 2017.

McKay, Andrew. *Russell Westbrook: The Inspirational Story Behind One of Basketball's Premier Point Guards*. Digital edition. Morrisville, NC: Lulu Press, 2016.

Redban, Bill. *Russell Westbrook: The Inspirational Story of Basketball Superstar Russell Westbrook*. Seattle, WA: CreateSpace Independent Publishing Platform, 2014.

**On the Internet**

Russell Westbrook. ESPN
http://www.espn.com/nba/player/stats/_/id/3468/russell-westbrook

Russell Westbrook. nba.com
http://www.nba.com/players/russell/westbrook/201566

Russell Westbrook Why Not? Foundation
http://rwwhynotfoundation.org/

**Works Consulted**

Allen, Percy. "Sonics take UCLA's Russell Westbrook with the No. 4 draft pick." *Seattle Times*, June 27, 2008. http://www.seattletimes.com/sports/nba/sonics-take-uclas-russell-westbrook-with-the-no-4-draft-pick/

Baldwin, Mike. "Thunder guard Russell Westbrook makes All-Rookie team." *NewsOK*, May 1, 2009. http://newsok.com/article/3365738

Brunt, Cliff. "OKC's Westbrook proving he is MVP candidate, great teammate." Yahoo Sports, April 3, 2017. https://sports.yahoo.com/news/okcs-westbrook-proving-mvp-candidate-great-teammate-190520808--nba.html

Clarke, Khari. "The Oklahoma City Thunder Were Very, Very Close to Passing on Russell Westbrook." *The Source*, May 25, 2016. http://thesource.com/2016/05/25/the-oklahoma-city-thunder-were-very-very-close-to-passing-on-russell-westbrook/

Guardabascio, Mike. "Russell Westbrook's Story Is Quintessential Long Beach." *Grunion Gazette Newspaper*, July 23, 2012. http://www.gazettes.com/sports/feature-russell-westbrook-s-story-is-quintessential-long-beach/article_8c544144-d559-11e1-8c3e-001a4bcf887a.html

Jenkins. Lee. "Russell Westbrook: 'I Was Never Going to Lead.'" *Sports Illustrated*, October 20, 2016. https://www.si.com/nba/2016/10/19/russell-westbrook-thunder-nba-season-preview-kevin-durant

Jenkins, Lee. "The Value of Zero Is Increasing." *The New York Times*, March 15, 2007. http://www.nytimes.com/2007/03/15/sports/ncaabasketball/15zero.html?pagewanted=print

MacMahon, Tim. "Russell Westbrook caps historic season with 42nd triple-double." ESPN, April 10, 2017. http://www.espn.com/nba/story/_/id/19120414/oklahoma-city-thunder-russell-westbrook-sets-nba-record-42nd-triple-double-season

Markazi, Arash. "Westbrook: The honor guard." ESPN, April 30, 2010. http://www.espn.com/los-angeles/nba/columns/story?id=5150492

Mayberry, Darnell. "Russell Westbrook's journey from community center gyms to the NBA All-Star game." *NewsOK*, February 19, 2011. http://newsok.com/article/3542475

Neuharth-Keusch, A.J. "Russell Westbrook could make All-Star Game history Sunday night." *USA Today*, February 19, 2017. http://www.usatoday.com/story/sports/nba/allstar/2017/02/19/russell-westbrook-nba-all-star-game-mvp/98135228/

Palmer, Chris. "From the Bottom to the Top: The Russell Westbrook Story." *Bleacher Report*, November 12, 2015. http://bleacherreport.com/articles/2587948-from-the-bottom-to-the-top-the-russell-westbrook-story

Piellucci, Mike. "'I Believe that Khelcey's Energy Is Inside Russell': The Legacy of Khelcey Barrs." Vice Sports, April 14, 2017. https://sports.vice.com/en_us/article/russell-westbrook-the-legacy-of-khelcey-barrs

Riley, Daniel. "Why Not Russell Westbrook?" *GQ*, October 2016. http://www.gq.com/story/russell-westbrook-thunder-profile

Robertson, Oscar. "Oscar Robertson is NOT hating that Westbrook broke his triple-double record." The Undefeated, April 9, 2017. https://theundefeated.com/features/oscar-robertson-westbrook-broke-triple-double-record/

Schilken, Chuck. "Russell Westbrook makes largest donation ever to UCLA by a former Bruins basketball player." *Los Angeles Times*, December 14, 2015. http://www.latimes.com/sports/ucla/uclanow/la-sp-sn-russell-westbrook-ucla-donation-20151214-story.html